PROSOPOPOEIA FICTION

Letchumy Appavoo

MINERVA PRESS
ATLANTA LONDON SYDNEY

PROSOPOPOEIA FICTION
Copyright © Letchumy Appavoo 1999

All Rights Reserved

No part of this book may be reproduced in any form.
by photocopying or by any electronic or mechanical means.
including information storage or retrieval systems.
without permission in writing from both the copyright owner
and the publisher of this book.

ISBN 0 75410 576 8

First Published 1999 by
MINERVA PRESS
315–317 Regent Street
London W1R 7YB

Printed in Great Britain for Minerva Press

PROSOPOPOEIA FICTION

*To my late parents,
Mr and Mrs Candasamy Appavoo,
my colleagues, friends and relatives
all over the world*

Contents

One	The Haunting Hand	7
Two	Furnished Commodes of the Past	13
Three	Effective Appealing Healing	16
Four	Arjuna the Thunder God	19
Five	Lucky Legs	21
Six	The Casket	22
Seven	Mrs Death	24
Eight	Superstition	25
Nine	Casual Conversation	26
Ten	Smoking Taxi	28
Eleven	Operation Frog	29
Twelve	Two Mediums If You Please	31
Thirteen	Garden Scenes	35
Fourteen	The Curse of the Elder Tree	37

The Haunting Hand

His body faced the east to grace the summer sunshine, a perfect day was born whereby his home held the beauty of an elegant cottage, portrayed exactly as the architect had had in his mind when he was building.

Funnily enough, the owner was a man of changeable moods and integrity, although unfortunately partially educated due to monetary circumstances in his family background. His true potential was degradingly limited, through no fault of his own. However, determination like procrastination is the thief of time, progress in one's own soul helped him to climb the ladder of success. This man whom we shall name as Rupert Crust was a very keen gardener, he placed every article in plant life absolutely perfectly like most schizophrenics becoming quite possessed with the colour scene in his mind. Once his green garden was perfected, he had pillars built on each side of his garden, with seating, Roman and Grecian vases, which he collected from antique shops.

The whole set up was a delightful sight, indescribable. Being quite possessed with possessions made Mr Crust rather possessive, such people become very difficult to live with.

The next craze beset him, he wanted a piano and a good comfortable double bed with mattress. Money was no object, simply because it was for his own personal use. What a man! He thought every plan out in advance, which included his will which he drew up in the presence of his solicitor, he had no living relatives, and thus charities such as hospitals, Salvation Army, animal welfare, churches and musical societies were the beneficiaries, just in order to see his name engraved onto a plaque. What a show-off even at or after death.

Soon after Mr Crust had made his will, he passed away peacefully in his sleep, i.e. upon his new bed and mattress which were too comfortably healthful. Why! No exercise.

This is where this story begins. Mr Rupert Crust hid a lot of coins and items in his piano body work, he felt it was safer than a bank. Well! Quite frankly it shows you, the reader, how wrong he was. When his cottage was sold a middle-aged couple bought it, and were absolutely delighted with its tasteful picturesque garden and lovely toned piano. They bought the furniture with it.

As months passed by hauntings started to haunt the house, I mean cottage of course!

In no time the cottage was sold and passed through eight home owners. Alas! each keeping silent prior to the sales, in case of restricting the sale of the cottage.

Mr and Mrs Kitburn, also a middle-aged couple, bought the property. They occupied it for four years. The reason for selling was quite unbelievable. Mr Crust was haunting his cottage, he could not rest because of the capital he had left hidden in the piano.

One night as Mrs Kitburn was asleep, old Crusty placed his cold, in fact ice-cold, hand upon her ankle and pulled it with all his ghostly might, he then pulled her leg and dislocated her hip, rendering her as a cripple, so an appointment was arranged at the local hospital for a hip replacement. I ask you, who would, or possibly could, believe this?

Well! It did happen. Then Mr and Mrs Kitburn sold the cottage, lock, stock and barrel to a spinster, who only used it at weekends, because she resided at her work-place where they accommodated staff.

One weekend the spinster Miss Anna Jones decided to play the piano where she went to relax at the cottage. A funny incident took place, a hand which she could not see but felt. Yes! It was invisible all right! It gripped her hand tightly, grasping it very tight as if to stop her playing the instrument. So she slapped it, the blow was hard intentionally, but she never felt any hurt on her hand from the slap. *How strange*! she thought, but carried on playing the piano. Ah! but Mr Crust's ghostly tricks went much further, he grasped her thigh with a vengeance. Because she could not see anything or anybody, she spoke up.

'Who are you, and what is it that troubles you?'

Of course there was no reply. In her mind it daunted her that the piano was haunted. Needless to say she became agitated. If anyone had heard her talking to an open space or to herself as it appeared, definitely, she would have to be classified as insane or going off the top!

When bedtime arrived Miss Jones decided to use the double bed and mattress, which she had never used before, but inherited with the purchase of the cottage. There she lay in quiet solitude for one hour, the grandfather clock striking the midnight hour. As spooky events took over, note well, her lights were switched off. The cold hand grasped her foot, then upwards towards her leg pulling her leg downwards within the bed, she moved with the pull of the hand. The light went on of its own accord.

Miss Jones by this time was perspiring profusely saying, 'Stop it! Who are you, why can't you rest in peace, you evil soul?'

Still, no reply. Once more, Rupert Crust's hand grasped her ankle with a jerk, she saved her bones from dislocating or breaking, by simply moving with the manoeuvres of the ghostly hand. It gave her the shivers up her spinal column. *Who is this creature, spirit or demon?* she thought.

As she could not sleep, she shifted out of that room, into another bed until daylight peered through her windows, bringing a new day, with mysterious thoughts rambling through her confused brain.

She bathed, dressed and prayed, then went out for a walk, en route she met her new neighbours, they were elderly ladies, two in number, very friendly and talkative. They asked Miss Jones how she found her lovely cottage. Then Miss Jones opened up her heart relating to them the ordeal she encountered, telling them about the hand, well in fact the whole episode.

The two old ladies were not surprised. They glanced at each other, the eldest said, 'Shall we tell her what we know?'

'Yes, of course,' said the younger of the two.

'Well! You see it's like this, my dear young lady, we don't want to scare you. Before you bought the cottage there were eight previous owners, look at your house deeds. The last owner was a Mrs Kitburn who went through the same ordeal as you are going through now. Only she became a cripple, the ghost's hand dislocated her hip, she had to go to the hospital and fix it up, then she and her old man made off to Wales.'

Having listened to the tale of the old dears. Miss Jones decided to defy the ghostly hand, went back to play the piano, and on each occasion, the ice cold grasp of old Crusty grew tighter and tighter. Miss Jones had no fear by this time, but was curious, so she went to the local priest of the Catholic faith and related the story to him. He did not ridicule her, but went along and performed an exorcism service, offering prayers to rest the soul in peace of Mr Rupert Crust.

However, sad to say, Crusty did not rest. Why? Eventually things became apparent, and the story fell into place, so read carefully now. Miss Jones had friends living abroad, they were getting married and wanted to come to England for their honeymoon. *Fine! Just the job,* she thought, *they can use this cottage, whilst I stay at my staff quarters.* The wedding took place abroad, and the couple flew over to Britain. Arrangements were made, Miss Jones met them at the airport, and as a wedding gift gave them the full run of the cottage, handing over the house keys, showing them how various gadgets worked etc. Then they bade each other farewell until they were to meet again.

Time passed on, the honeymoon couple became restless, argumentative, and quarrelled a lot. In fact the husband was rather brutal, he gave his wife a slap across the face. Why? You may ask. Yes! She saw a man in a white robe, with long white hair, and staring, ghostly, wicked, eyes, carrying a candlestick with holder and he sat at the piano, looking at it, quite possessed. Naturally, she screamed in absolute terror, her husband saw nothing and thought she was hysterical with hallucinations, because she had used sleeping pills.

When their honeymoon was nearing the end Miss Jones called in to visit them, and see how they were getting along. It was then that the young wife related the story to Miss Jones, who really pitied her friend, because her husband would not listen or tolerate such a story, which was a fact. He thought he had married a crank! Miss Jones, now completely convinced the place was haunted, went back to see the priest to whom she related the story. Once more, an exorcism was performed.

When the couple left for their homeland, Miss Jones decided to stay at her work-accommodation, and a week later a little girl was looking for a piano, as she was interested in that instrument. Miss Jones being generous gave the piano as a gift to the little girl aged seven years, but transport arrangements were to be made by her parents. All was agreed and the girl sang and danced around with happiness as the very thought of owning a piano went to her head.

Time came for the haulage contractor to collect the piano, it literally took six men to lift the instrument onto the van, so one of the men said to Miss Jones, 'What have you got in here, is it a dead body?'

They both roared with laughter and off they all went with Mr Crust's piano, the little girl waiting anxiously at home. Miss Jones suddenly thought she should have chopped up the piano into bits, in order to see what it contained to make it so weighted. That is the mystery to this day.

Finally, the mattress and bed were burnt on Guy Fawkes Night. At last the cottage was at peace, absolute peace. Never let the haunting hand touch you! Did Rupert Crust go along with his piano, or did he enjoy his RIP?

Beware of that cottage, it is for sale now.

Furnished Commodes of the Past

She was rather an uncanny rich, beautiful, lazy old lady, who fell ill in her luxurious mansion in the West End of London. She had servants galore, but her needs were mainly practical items, including a jug with bowl for ablutions and a commode at the bedside, regardless of the most lovely bathroom and toilet she possessed.

Her family doctor was summoned to her bedside, as she had been feeling unwell for the past eight hours and the servants were worried, their job was at stake. What would happen if this old lady died? Sad for the under-privileged society as it may seem, one has a death date, not to mention that life ceases unawares to those who possess it; and so who are we, mere creatures of the earth, to meddle with it.

Dr Roger Aventum arrived late in the afternoon to find Lady Emily St Klere feeling weak and in bed, draped in satins, looking pale and lethargic. The doctor sat in the armchair next to her bed, whilst he extracted facts pertaining to her present illness. The two of them soon became carried away in conversation on daily topics over a cup of tea.

Suddenly Dr Aventum paused and stared around the room, which was very large; with Plaster of Paris ceiling, and flimsy drapes; he appeared to be dumbstruck by such a tastefully decorated room. Although he had known the elderly lady since he was a little boy, he had never been inside her bedroom. He asked her if she had a commode, as he felt that she should remain in her bedroom.

'Young man!' she retorted in an arrogant tone. 'You are sitting on it.' She became quite adamant of the idea that this young man, whom she knew as a little baby boy should be questioning her on personal matters pertaining to her home.

In a rage, she waved her walking stick in the air, like a crazy devil on heat.

She commanded him to be off, but stated, 'Before you go, leave me my medicine.'

The servants heard the din of her walking stick falling to the floor, and they rushed to the bedroom. He handed her some medication and was ushered out with one of the servants.

He left quietly.

Lady Emily St Klere passed peacefully away in bed during the early hours of that night; her favourite boy Doc. Roger was back again only to finalize her death certificate. There was much talk about the funeral she was endowed with, the best mahogany box, satin lined, and gold trimmings etc. Why? All this fussing, only to be placed in a hole where the grave digger had a task, even when work was restricted for the under-privileged class. However poor he may seem, he would never be really short or out of work in those dire circumstances where vicars and parasitical friends encroach to enjoy the last rites, hoping to obtain her wealth.

She was no fool to mankind, and shocked were they as the solicitor read her will and her black cat Binky got the lot. Lock stock and barrel and meals for life, with the rest going to the animal welfare hospital.

Dr Roger Aventum had a good laugh, and that is free of course! The servants were back to square one, looking for work.

Good luck to all of them, for they are blessed with good health, though definitely not wealth.

Effective Appealing Healing

Mr Butone fell madly in love. A floodgate of joy filled his heart, as he was ensconced by the beauty of her face, by the structure of her facial bones inundated with waves of indescribable eternal youth. She had a soft unblemished skin and the texture of her hair radiated the privilege of her background and her good diet.

Alas! Some uncouth scoundrel of society, obviously jealous, homeless, workless, perverted by usage of drugs wanted to cause a catastrophe involving hatred. For if you suffer from jealousy, you are self-centred, therefore mentally ill, and the most striking thing is that the molecular structure in a jealous person's brain cell is limited, just as if an electric drill has channelled its way – causing destruction, and imbecile-like behaviour patterns. The result is a wild schizophrenic on heat; wild but calm and pleasant to look at.

Think clearly now, what should you do? There are various aspects in order to deal with this matter. Lesson one is to keep level headed. Never allow the culprit to know that you are aware of his actions. Then follow on to the second lesson which is observation. Does this odd character use drugs, chemical sprays, radium or witchcraft?

The perverted idiot thinks on a lower intelligence plane, diverting his thoughts to the dead spirits and weird practices of the new age religious beliefs, what does he infiltrate when he prays? He never ever mentions God or Jesus Christ or Heaven.

Frankly, I think he is the Devil's partner, having defiled the Holy Oath and Prayer. Pity him for he knows nothing better in life. If he should die, I wonder where he is going?

Shall I tell you? The earth, limbo or hell – definitely not Heaven!

'Why speakest thou in riddles ye nomadic imp, does goodliness not thy life from Godliness skimp?'

This described evil-being had taken a photograph of the fine-featured lady, together with a doll and some pins, which he pricked from time to time, incanting words of black magic.

The evil-beings were a couple practising witchcraft, they were very interested in the Occult sciences, but would never admit to it. So one day their chosen victim fell ill with a swollen face which developed into a rash scarring the skin in several areas of the face, which was weeping with serum and pus leading to an infection of course.

The doctor was summoned to see the fine-featured lady, but he was unable to diagnose accurately, as he had never encountered sorcery. However, the victim attended a spiritualist church by invitation. Various mediums, clairvoyants and healers stated that the diagnosis was an act of evil witchcraft done by a neighbour. One of the mediums began to pray for guidance and spiritual healing. The healer touched the area of the face and head of the victim, saying prayers whilst tendering her healing touch which radiated a power of indescribable heat above body temperature followed by ice cold tremblings within the head and facial areas.

Within forty-eight hours, the victim's face was healed, back to her normal clear skin. Cured at last!

'So take heed,' said the healer, 'do not mix with witches and wizards.' The healer stated that you could return the sorcery to the sender by repeating daily the Lord's Prayer, and saying, 'Return to sender. I am cured! I am cured, so rest assured.'

As time passed the sorcerer and sorceress became unhappy, they did not notice each other or caress, and the rash filled their entire bodies and faces, as the ugliness of their souls turned them into gargoyles. How sad and bad, now they are both in a mental asylum, unable to communicate with God.

Remember, nothing is greater than God. So they all made the sign of the cross, i.e. the healed lady, the healer, mediums and spiritualists who were from the Christian Society.

Arjuna the Thunder God

He rode upon the clouds which carpeted the sky in beauteous splendour. The chariot led by six white stallions of the best breed. Of course! They were led by Arjuna himself, the King of Thunder, Lightning and Rain.

The chariot was built in pure silver and gold studs, and each time it rained and hailstones were falling, Arjuna was on his way to his castle in the heavens. Bang went the wheels of the chariot over the clouds, rain poured upon the earth below showering the people with great joy as the heavens opened up to endow the plants, insects and animal kingdom with the necessary essentials of life which is water, water and water everywhere.

As Arjuna was steering his way through the distant clouds, occasionally he used his whip to speed his chariot. Each time his whip struck lightning flashed down upon the earth's blue-rock. This can be very dangerous, seething through trees, making clear cuts, causing fires to trees, houses, cars, and even killing people or animal and plant life.

Civilized scientific society realized copper wire was a lightning conductor, and henceforth builders included copper-wiring to properties where lightning and thunder were prevalent.

All the Hindus prayed to Arjuna when rain poured upon them, because he was the King of the Clouds, Rain, Lightning and Thunder. Whenever they prayed they said, 'Arjuna, Arjuna, Arjuna! We thank thee for the water, but please spare us from your lightning whip, unless our time is up.'

God bless Arjuna, King of the Thunder and Clouds. Many decades passed the earth as it warmed up, moles and rats could not barely tolerate the heat underground. Unable to be sheltered too long they raised themselves to the surface, whilst Arjuna blessed them with water.

Each time the hailstones grew larger pelted down like shells from a gun. 'Ouch!' said the Bunny Rabbit. 'I think I'll sink into the earth rather than end up with a bruise on my skull.'

But before Mr Rabbit could retreat into the earth, a farmer grasped him by the ears, and enjoyed a good cooked rabbit stew for his supper.

Is there a safe place on earth or above in the clouds?

Arjuna God of Thunder and Rain will keep you moist and clean. For cleanliness is godliness and lightning a killer of evil!

Lucky Legs

One day whilst walking within the hospital grounds, the Sister, then entering a lounge through double doors, and passing a crowd of young inadequate girls in care. They sat in a circle, and greeted the Sister-in-Charge by saying, 'Good morning, Lucky Legs.'

A pause took place between the sister and the girls, the sister called out to one girl from the crowd and said, 'What is all that about?'

'Well, Miss, they say you are lucky your legs are not broken yet.'

The Sister laughed heartily, which irritated the girls immensely, because they expected to see the Sister upset and crying.

Replying the Sister stated, 'My legs are tough, they'll walk for ever and ever.'

Some laughed whilst others cried openly. Needless to mention the Sister was known as Sister Lucky Legs, and whenever they saw her approaching, they hurriedly grabbed dusters and brooms and looked as if they were busy working.

A joke is a joke, and laughter is a cure, so enjoy the situation as it arises.

The Casket

Rebecca was a pleasant old lady from a working class family, her tasks were mopping the floors, washing dishes etc.

The weather was extremely hot, and Rebecca had been over-worked during that summer season, her employer was Lady Florinda Broad.

Rebecca had enjoyed her tasks in the employment of Lady Florinda for the past ten years.

It was therefore inevitable that Rebecca had lived her span of life, which was now coming to a close; yes, it was a heart attack.

She dropped to the ground, and drew her last breath with a sigh of relief and a face filled with god-like happiness, as she hallucinated and stated she saw angels. Her complexion faded within hours as the oxygen ceased and expelled from her living to dying body.

Death faced the onlookers, with great sadness, whilst her soul wended away from the world. Peace at last!

Dear Rebecca was cremated, her ashes placed in a casket made of pure silver, which was sent to her sister's home, whereby the family were to decide the site for rest. In the meantime her sister Mary placed the casket upon the top kitchen shelf.

The family members were to arrive that day, for the necessary arrangements. Ah! What a task.

Anyway, Mary's son came home and made himself very useful. As he loved cooking, he decided to make a stew, so off to the kitchen he enlightened himself to his culinary delight.

He chopped the various vegetables and meat to the required size, found a suitably sized pot, proceeded to cook, and he grasped the casket not knowing the contents, and thinking it was pepper, he added some to his stew, and replaced the casket on the shelf.

The food smelled good, the aroma wafted in the breeze, making every member in the household hungry. Dinner was served, with nothing left over. Coffee and conversation after dinner.

Mary's son Don, in the course of chatting about the past and remembrances of his favourite Aunt Rebecca, asked where they had placed her ashes.

His mother replied, 'Aunty Rebecca is on the kitchen shelf. Did you see the silver casket?'

'What happened to Aunt Rebecca, was she not buried?'

'Oh! didn't you know? I put her on the shelf in the kitchen to rest, until I can find a nice place, her ashes are in the silver casket.

'Goodness, gracious, how on earth did you leave her in the kitchen on the shelf, I used her in the stew as pepper, mother!'

'Never mind son,' said his mother, 'at least we all know where she is, and is likely to be expelled, from the human bowels to the earth where she dwelt, so we'll all have a dose of castor oil. From earth to dust, may her soul rest in peace, by the grace of our Lord almighty.'

Mrs Death

As the sea gushed against the cliffs, it rolled and roared and hissed as it settled back into the ocean.

A busy clinic was in progress at a seaside town hospital outpatient department. The staff nurse was calling out names of patients for the doctor to interview, she raises her voice to be heard, holding her notes towards her chest.

'Next!... Mrs Death.'

A stout lady in a fur coat, and high-heeled shoes, gets up from her chair, swaying her hips to and fro, almost positively to attract attention to her fur coat.

Closely passing the staff nurse she whispers in anger, 'The name is Dee Aarth, if you please,' and she rushed away into the doctor's surgery, complaining about the ignorant nurse.

The staff nurse who was bewildered because she only pronounced names according to their spelling, and not origin of abode. *Why make a mountain out of a molehill?* she thought. Surely the English dictionary is the guide for pronunciation on that score. Poor staff nurse, she is tough, remember, your sympathy is not a necessity, she can cope with insults, indifferences and hypocrisy. That's what nursing does for you!

Superstition

Three boys varying in ages from ten to eighteen years were extremely restless and aggressive, due to their dietary intake. The wrong foodstuff again! What did they eat? Beef ah! – infected with some mad cow disease, or just a plain excuse for their frustration, with nobody to support their energies, and to improve their speech, or even listening to them. Every child or person needs someone to listen to them. So please give them a hearing ear. If for some reason or ignorance there is parental negligence, your listening is their aid.

Well! One day they became difficult characters, something was troubling them, so they took their tantrums and became destructive towards property i.e. smashing walls, ruining gardens and thieving anything within sight.

One day the owner of the property saw the thugs breaking her wall, so in order to scare them off, she pretended to be a witch, and said:

'I curse you for breaking my wall, so your legs will break just like you've broken my wall.'

Suddenly, they became hyperactive, and replaced all the brickwork to its normal position.

Unfortunately, one of the lads met with a car accident within a fortnight, he broke his legs, had crutches, and believed it was the curse for breaking the wall.

Please rest assured, never be superstitious, there was never a curse in the first place. Silly you! That was coincidence!

Casual Conversation

Area:

Waiting room in casualty out-patient department.
   Nurse places wheelchair with patient, in a corner of space left.
   Instruction to patient, 'Please do not drink or eat anything, until you have seen the doctor.'
   Two youths walk into casualty, one with an eye injury, the other to be reviewed. Everyone was quiet. In order to break the stillness, one of the youths offers the patient in the wheelchair, 'Would you like a drink, dearie?'
   Reply from the old lady, 'Yes, me lad, I'd love one, son.'
   The nurse interrupts stating to the old lady, 'No! You cannot have a drink, I've already told you.'
   The patient replies to the lad, 'I don't know what all the fuss is about, but I've got a hell of a lot of whisky in me bag, and that is why I'm here in the first place.'
   Then she goes on to say, 'You see I slipped and fell, so they're only going to check me bones, which ain't broken.'
   The boys were smiling.
   Then the conversation between the boys and the lady continues, 'I had an awful queer year, it seems as if it is going to be the same again this year.'
   With that message she lets the boy know her age, 'I'm seventy-seven years old you know.'

Boy replies: 'No, Gran, I never would have guessed it, I only took you for thirty years old.' He had a sly grin, which she detected but said nothing.

Smoking Taxi

Scene:

In the out-patient waiting room, there are many patients waiting to be seen. Patient is leaving hospital after she was attended, rings for a taxi-cab, she is extremely deaf, with a cigarette dangling from her lips, and is ignorant not to notice the non-smoking sign.

'Can I have a smoking taxi, please?'

The other patients in the waiting room were in fits of laughter, because her voice was raised, and the replying voice was loud too! Voice from taxi rank replies:

'Madam, do you want me to set it alight before I get there? Where are you going please?'

Deaf woman replies:

'Just get here, lad, and you'll find out.'

At least her smoking taxi kept the patients amused, with a topic of conversation for the day.

Operation Frog

How perfect and glorious the day appeared; sunshine, lovely temperature; tolerable and peaceful thoughts wafting in the breeze.

A gifted doctor set up in practice in the countryside, he had a tall stature, with a smooth tanned skin, handsome features with very expressive eyes that almost peered into your soul. This doctor could diagnose accurately, what more could you ask for in a country practice?

One of the local farmers came along to see the doctor.

'Doctor,' he said, 'I know I have got a frog in my tummy, he jumps up and down, even if I sit or sleep or eat.'

'Burp! Burp! Burp!' gulped the farmer in the presence of the doctor.

'Did you hear that? Can you help me, sir?'

The doctor, not amazed, realized he was dealing with a psychiatric patient, he respected his patient's views, in order to give them confidence and reassurance.

After ten sessional interviews with the farmer the doctor discussed possible surgery.

The doctor said, 'The frog will be removed at the earliest possible moment.' So the necessary forms were signed and held in abeyance.

Dr Kukoo wended his way into the city, there he searched for a living frog in a local pet shop. He bought it and brought it in a jar to his surgery where it was hidden in a cupboard.

The farmer patient was gowned and capped for operation and wheeled on the trolley to theatre. The preparation arrangement with the staff was a sworn secret. The farmer was given a sleeping pill, and whilst in his sleep state, a black biro pen was used to appear as a cut with sutures on his abdomen, a dressing applied over it. In other words a scar of three inches' length, with no actual cut or operation was carried out.

When the farmer woke up, Dr Kukoo showed him the live frog in the jar, and said, 'Here is the frog. I removed from your tummy, you can take it home with you.'

The patient was completely relieved, in fact cured.

'What are you going to call your frog, sir?'

'Well,' said the patient, 'how about Fred!'

'Fine,' said the doctor. 'Do not touch your scar or wash your abdomen for three days, then nurse will remove the dressing, and you will not even bear a scar.'

Needless to say, the nurse washed the abdomen and great joy filled the face of the farmer.

Two Mediums If You Please

It was a bleak night, the snow falling, ice cold weather, everyone out of sight, either in bed or near their fires.

Miss Gag was on her way to visit her sick father, using her scooter. Unfortunately the scooter hit a rock, and threw Miss Gag forward, hitting her head and other parts of her body. She was already a handicapped person with deformed limbs and distorted finger joints.

A couple in the neighbourhood heard the crash and cries for help, they ran out of their front door and found Miss Gag in a state of blood and agony. Mr Jelly picked her up into his arms, and carried her into his house, they looked up into one another's eyes. Yes, it was love at first sight, so she said.

They gave her warmth and a drink, and the ambulance took her to the local hospital. Mr Jelly accompanied her, but Mrs Jelly remained at home. How very kind.

Weeks went by, whilst Miss Gag was recovering in hospital, Mr Jelly visited her without fail, his wife helped with her laundry and toiletries. When Miss Gag was discharged, Mr Jelly accompanied her home, this was their destiny, she invited him to tea, and as time passed they became incessantly closer until they grew into lovers, cheating Mrs Jelly of her husband's affection.

Mr Jelly and Miss Gag practised clairvoyance and mediumship, they thought they were great spiritualists, who could foretell your whole future. In my opinion they were liars, confidence tricksters ruthless to make money, not comprehending the subject. They founded a church for their racket, where they were to hide loot and abusing Mr Jelly's wife's capital, as a result Mrs Jelly drowned her sorrows with drink. She liked wines and sherries, and became an alcoholic, how sad to destroy a sober person into a state of utter depression. Why did Miss Gag do it? She said Mr Jelly said she was the most beautiful woman he had ever seen.

Well! The verdict is yours.

Beauty is to the beholder of course. All I could say was, I think he needs his eyes tested, don't you? Mr Jelly was a deceptive creature of the demons, he took this woman's confidence, and abused her for as long as he wanted as he received with gratitude, in her very own accommodation.

Does one have to be bound with such gratitude? Lover or no lover. She was a person who never could say 'no' everything was 'yes please'. Whilst her life petered into sexual diseases, wafting a stench of each type in the breeze. How can a woman do this to herself lest she be an imbecile. Be gone dull care, I pray thee be gone from me!

Beware, for the wrath of God did catch up on him, he developed an infection as a result of his association, and had to be hospitalized and abstain from men or women, for reasons best known to him and his lover.

She only used married men who abused her by cheating and praising her as a beauty, as if she were the Goddess Venus. Not being unduly unkind, a gargoyle would have been an appropriate match. I sometimes wonder if these are cursed people, for ugliness is considered as part of evil, especially, if you are not born pretty.

Mr Jelly returns to Mrs Jelly he pretends to be a great affectionate husband, whilst he was still visiting Miss Gag there was no further bodily involvement.

This two-timing man had both women crazily in love with him, but was like a mute, he could not perform. His lover cried and became depressed as a result, his wife was relieved to abstain.

He lied to his lover, he said he was going to get a divorce and marry her, but he is just waiting for his wife to take the action, as she was the person with money, because divorces cost a lot of money.

So his lover decided she could not wait, and stated to him that his wife was an alcoholic and it would be easy to get rid of her. So Miss Gag was on drugs for her injury condition, and decided to crush her pills into Mrs Jelly's bottle of sherry and wine, enough to kill. Mr Jelly put the bottle into his wife's wine cabinet, note well, Mr Jelly is teetotal, here is where the crime ripens.

Mr Jelly goes to work as usual, he is a security guard at a bank, and his lover does not work, as she is classified as handicapped. Mrs Jelly is very friendly with her neighbours, she invites the next door neighbour for a drink. He is an ambulance driver, he was off duty, and agreed to have the drink. She poured him a glass of sherry, and poured one for herself. The ambulance driver drank his first, as Mrs Jelly made sandwiches, but when she returned with the treats she found the ambulance driver on the floor, in agony, holding his abdomen. She immediately called for an ambulance to take him to the local hospital, he had a stomach washout, and Mrs Jelly got the blame for administering drugs, although she definitely was innocent.

By the luck of the draw the villain, Mr Jelly, returned to hear the story of the ambulance driver in hospital, immediately Mr Jelly cleared the poison drink bottles, and then replaced it with clear drinks. He poured it out on to the soil in the garden and turned it over with a spade.

Since the episode, Mrs Jelly became teetotal, but never ever discovered the truth of the matter. In fact Mrs Jelly was naive of her husband's affair, and he acted as an affectionate husband should. Suddenly, he came to his senses and gave up his lover, whom he used as his plaything. Never to be seen again.

My advice is: never take a drink whether it be two mediums or one.

Garden Scenes

Perched upon the apple tree is a cockatoo who makes a sound as if he is saying, 'How do you do?'

My garden is quite picturesque in the summer, it has many shrubs, roses and fruit, a few bulbs and creepers around the place, a lawn with laid paths requiring a lot of work, and skill to display a colour scheme. In the garden is a large humming bee, who flutters around whilst pollinating the plants. If you study the bumble bee, he is pretty and thinks he owns the area he works in.

There are squirrels, they jump as if they have ballet shoes, then sit up chewing nuts, sharing the birds' food.

Now, in Cheshire, we have magpies. They are the thieving birds, they are quite handsome birds to see, looks to me as if they are in top and tails, like an evening suit, black jacket and white shirt, with a tinge of shiny blue or silver on the wing as it spreads.

One morning, whilst feeding the birds with crusts of bread and rice, I saw a bird, it was out of the ordinary, yes, a cross-bred bird with the body of a brown dove and wings of a magpie. I was very tempted to photograph it, but it cleared off before I could get my camera.

Lots of other species of birds come to dine at my garden, I do encourage them, they get their food and water daily.

Unfortunately, we have cats roaming around, viciously attacking the birds, they seem to prowl around, pouncing upon the dear birds, showing off, as if they had the authority to do so. I have deemed them as vicious murderers.

Instead of catching the English rats they are feasting on the birds, these birds require help. Grasped and feathered, half naked they flee, watching out for human help. They know they will get it.

The Curse of the Elder Tree

Pigeons are great carriers of plants and vegetation.

One day as the sun shone brightly, the owner of a homing pigeon felt that his pigeon needed exercising, so he opened the cage and gave the bird the freedom of the air. You could hear the fluttering of its wings, as it wended its way up towards the sky, despite the propelling noise of a jet aeroplane passing over the clouds. The bird experienced challenge and loved it. Courage embarked within the soul of this bird, it never took off in flight with fright, this held the owner's delight.

Suddenly the pigeon must have perched itself upon an elderberry tree in the neighbourhood, and gathered some seedlings on its feet, before dropping the seeds in a garden. The tree grew rapidly, filling the garden space with its trunk and many leaves, not mentioning the branches and bunches of elderflower, which is used in the composition of effective medicine and the berries used for wine making. Not a pleasant smelling tree.

There is a superstition attached to the elderberry tree:

'He who chops the elderberry tree, is one to be cursed and never will be free, and as a result may die within the days of three.'

So beware my friend, if your life is at an end, it may come sooner than you think.

Please save the tree, and God bless thee.